HORRIBLE HARRIET

written and illustrated by

Leigh HOBBS

ALLEN&UNWIN

For
Erica Wagner,
Coral Tulloch and Kersti Elliott

First published in 2001

Allen & Unwin
83 Alexander Street
Crows Nest NSW 2065
Australia
Phone: (61 2) 8425 0100
Fax: (61 2) 9906 2218
Email: info@allenandunwin.com
Web: http://www.allenandunwin.com

National Library of Australia
Cataloguing-in-Publication entry:

Hobbs, Leigh.
Horrible Harriet.
ISBN 1 86508 439 5 (hbk)
ISBN 1 86508 440 9.
I. Title.
A823.3

Set in 20 pt Bembo by Sandra Nobes
Designed by Sandra Nobes and Leigh Hobbs
Printed in China by Everbest Printing Co

10 9 8 7 6 5 4 3 2 1

Horrible Harriet lived at school.
She had a nest, high up in the roof.

Every morning, Harriet came down to attend class
and hand in her homework.
Her teacher, Mr Boggle, couldn't see very well –
he thought she was a good girl.

She was helpful too. When someone was naughty,
Harriet *always* told Mr Boggle.

'Why can't there be *more* students like Helpful Harriet?'
he often asked.

But everyone else thought that one Harriet
was quite enough. For as soon as Mr Boggle
turned his back, she was well and truly . . .

CRUEL and WICKED.

Not surprisingly, Horrible Harriet
sat alone at lunchtimes. She loved to cook,
and her tasty meals took a lot of planning.

Every afternoon,
when Mr Boggle and the children had gone home,

Horrible Harriet attended to her after-school chores.
There were teachers to be fed.

They lived in the cellar . . .

. . . and did Horrible Harriet's homework.
Mr Scruffy looked after her maths,
while Miss Plume took care of everything else.

She'd been there for years and had even grown
a wonderful little garden, full of plants that liked the dark.

If homework was late,
Horrible Harriet cracked her whip.

This made Mr Scruffy hurry,
but Miss Plume just growled
and hissed.

One day,
a new boy came to school.

His name was Athol Egghead and he was very polite.
'How do you do?' he said, when introduced to the class.

Athol found making friends difficult.
He was a shy boy, and was used to being overlooked.

When Mr Boggle asked for
someone to take care of him,
Horrible Harriet was quick
to volunteer.

'Splendid!' said Mr Boggle.
'I know you'll make Athol
feel *very* welcome.'

Naturally, Horrible Harriet made sure Athol's
first day was memorable.

In fact, she wanted to make it a day Athol would never forget.
When he lost his lunch . . .

Horrible Harriet insisted that he try her bat-ear
and monster-tail soup. 'Hmm, not bad,' said Athol.

After lunch, Athol met a charming chicken.

'Why, Miss Chicken,' said Athol, polite as ever,
'How nice of you to join me.'

Miss Chicken was speechless.

In the morning, Horrible Harriet found a lovely card on her desk. *Thank you for a wonderful day*, it said, *from A. Egghead*.

'I knew you were just the one to welcome the new boy,' said Mr Boggle.

It was a proud moment for Horrible Harriet.

Not long after that, Harriet showed Athol some bold new
steps when he joined her for dancing lessons.

Then, in art class, Athol Egghead
helped Harriet with her self-portrait.
'More pink in the cheeks,'
he suggested.

Harriet and Athol were having a marvellous time.

But, down in the cellar,
Mr Scruffy and Miss Plume
were growing restless.

They were on emergency rations. Mr Scruffy had raided
his secret chocolate supply, while Miss Plume
had to make do with spare homework.

One lunchtime, Athol had bad news.
'I must leave,' he said quietly.

Then he gave her a special gift, a painting, signed:
For my friend, Harriet.

When the time came, Harriet was very sad to see him go.

So she locked herself away for five whole days.

But, on the sixth day,
Harriet remembered . . .

There was work
to be done.

There were teachers
to be fed.

She had to get out and keep an eye on things.

Her old friends had been neglected.

Mr Boggle was certainly glad to see her back.
'If only there were more students like Harriet,'
he said to the class.

But everyone else thought that *one* Horrible Harriet
was *MORE* than enough.